PETE AND THE NORTH WIND

Retold from the Norse tale *The Lad Who Went to the North Wind*

Retold by FREYA LITTLEDALE   **Illustrated by TROY HOWELL**

SCHOLASTIC INC.

New York   Toronto   London   Auckland   Sydney

ISBN 0-590-40629-9

Text copyright © 1971 by Freya Littledale.
Illustrations copyright © 1988 by Troy Howell.
All rights reserved. Published by Scholastic Inc.
Art direction/design by Diana Hrisinko.

12 11 10 9 8 7 6 5 4 3   9/8 0 1 2 3/9

Printed in the U.S.A.   23

FIRST SCHOLASTIC PRINTING, MARCH 1988

For Bonnie Bryant

−*F.L.*

For Johnny

−*T.H.*

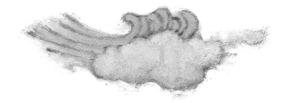

NCE THERE WAS a boy called Peter
who lived with his poor old mother.
One day Peter went to the barn
to get some flour.
But the North Wind came
and blew the flour away.

"The North Wind can't stop me," said Peter.
"We need flour to make our bread.
I will get more flour."
And he did.

But the North Wind blew
again…
and again.
And soon all the flour was gone.

"Well!" said Peter.
"I will find the North Wind
and get back our flour!"
So he said good-bye to his mother
and away he went.

He walked
and he walked
and he walked.
At last he found the North Wind.
"Good day," said Peter.

"Good day," said the North Wind.
"Why have you come to see me?"

"We are very poor," said Peter.
"And you blew away our flour.
  Please give it back."

"I don't have your flour," said the North Wind.
"But I will give you a magic cloth.
  Just say, 'Cloth, give me food,'
  and you will have all the food you want."

"Thank you," said Peter.
"I will take the cloth."
  And off he went.

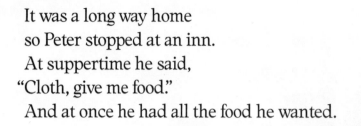

It was a long way home
so Peter stopped at an inn.
At suppertime he said,
"Cloth, give me food."
And at once he had all the food he wanted.

The innkeeper saw all the good food.
He looked at the cloth.
Ah, he thought,
that is a magic cloth.
I must have it for myself.

Late that night
the innkeeper went into Peter's room.
He stole the magic cloth
and put another in its place.

The next morning
Peter woke up.
He took the cloth
and went home to his mother.
"The North Wind is very nice," said he.
"He gave me a magic cloth."

"What good is a cloth?" asked Peter's mother.
"What can it do?"

"Just say, 'Cloth, give me food,'
and you will have all the food you want."

"Show me," said his mother.

So Peter put the cloth on the table and said,
"Cloth, give me food."
But the cloth did nothing.

"Hmmmmm," said Peter's mother.

"Well," said Peter,
"this is no magic cloth!
I will go back to the North Wind and tell him."

So he said good-bye to his mother
and off he went.

He walked
and he walked
and he walked.
Late in the day he found the North Wind.

"You blew away our flour," said Peter.
"And you gave me a magic cloth instead.
But the cloth is no good.
I want the flour back, please."

"I have no flour," said the North Wind.
"But I will give you a magic goat.
Just say, 'Goat, goat, make gold,'
and you will have all the gold you need."

"Thank you," said Peter.
"I will take the goat."
And he went on his way home.

But it was very late
so Peter stopped at the inn.

"Pay now," said the innkeeper.

"Very well," said Peter.
And he turned to the goat and said,
"Goat, goat, make gold."

At once, gold coins fell from the goat's mouth.
Peter patted the goat
and gave the coins to the innkeeper.

Ah, thought the innkeeper,
that is a magic goat.
I must have it for myself.

That night
when Peter was asleep,
the innkeeper went into Peter's room.
He stole the magic goat
and put another in its place.

The next morning
Peter woke up.
He took the goat
and went home to his mother.

"The North Wind is very nice," he told her.
"He gave me a magic goat."

"What can the goat do?" asked his mother.

"Just say, 'Goat, goat, make gold,'
and you will have all the gold you need."

"Show me," said his mother.

So Peter called the goat and said,
"Goat, goat, make gold."
The goat looked at Peter.
It looked at Peter's mother.
But it did not make gold.

"Hmmmmmmmmmmm," said Peter's mother.

"Well," said Peter,
"this is no magic goat!
I must go back to the North Wind and tell him."
So he said good-bye to his mother
and off he went.

He walked
and he walked
and he walked.
And he found the North Wind.

"You took our flour," said Peter.
"And you gave me a magic cloth.
But the cloth was no good.
So you gave me a magic goat.
But the goat is no good.
Give me back the flour, please."

"I don't have your flour," said the North Wind.
"I don't have another magic cloth.
I don't have another magic goat.
All I have left is a magic stick.
When you say, 'Hit, stick, hit,'
it will hit until you say, 'Stop, stick, stop.'"

"Will the magic stick help me?" asked Peter.

"It will," said the North Wind.

Peter thought and he thought and he thought—
The magic cloth gave food at the inn.
But it gave no food at home.

The magic goat gave gold at the inn.
But it gave no gold at home.

The innkeeper saw the magic cloth.
The innkeeper saw the magic goat....

At last Peter said, "You are right.
I will take the magic stick.
Thank you very much."
And off he went.

On the way home
Peter stopped at the inn.
The innkeeper saw the stick in Peter's hand.
Ah, he thought,
that must be a magic stick.
I will have it for myself.

That night Peter put the stick beside his bed.
He closed his eyes.
But he did not sleep.

He waited.
Soon the innkeeper opened Peter's door.
He walked to Peter's bed.
He touched the magic stick
and--

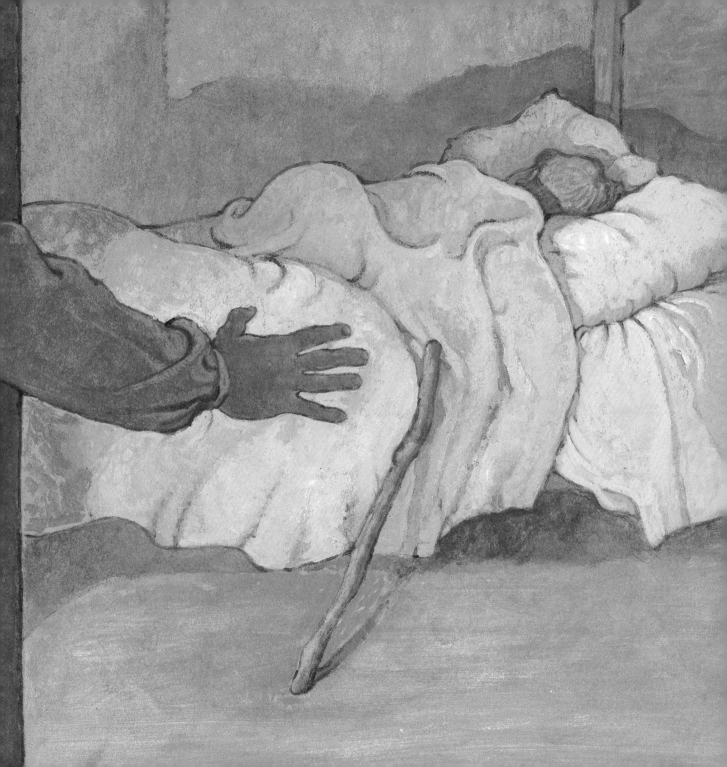

Peter opened his eyes.
"Hit, stick, hit," he said.
And the stick hit the innkeeper
on the ears,
on the nose,
on the mouth.
It hit his hands
and his feet
and his back.

The innkeeper jumped on a chair.
He yelled, "Oh my, oh my, oh my!
Make the stick stop!"

But the stick did not stop.

"Tell it to stop," cried the innkeeper.
"I will give you back the magic cloth.
I will give you back the magic goat.
But make the stick stop
or it will kill me!"

"Very well," said Peter.
"Stop, stick, stop."
And at once the stick stopped hitting the innkeeper.

The next morning
Peter went home to his mother.
The magic stick was in his hand.
The magic cloth was in his pocket.
And the magic goat was by his side.

From that day on,
the cloth gave them food,
the goat gave them gold,
and the stick did
just as it was told.